Meet Burback!

EDDIE SMITH

Copyright © **2026**

EDDIE SMITH

ISBN

978-1-971866-21-5

978-1-971866-22-2

978-1-971866-23-9

All Rights Reserved. Any unauthorized reprint or use of this material is strictly prohibited. No part of this book may be reproduced or transmitted in any form or by any means, electronic or mechanical, including photocopying, recording, or by any information storage and retrieval system without express written permission from the author.

All reasonable attempts have been made to verify the accuracy of the information provided in this publication. Nevertheless, the author assumes no responsibility for any errors and/or omissions.

DEDICATION

This book is dedicated to my loving wife, whose patience, encouragement, and belief in me year after year finally brought this story and this character I created with my daughters into print.

It is also dedicated to my two beautiful daughters, who made their dad proud when they were the age written in these pages, and who continue to make me proud as the women they have become — now sharing "Burback" with their own children."

A long time ago, in 1984, I worked in a big, creaky building.
My daughters loved to visit me there.

Every time they came,
they asked,
"Daddy, what's in the
basement?"

SERVICE ELEVATOR

I always said, "Just boxes.
Just tools."
But they didn't believe me.

One day I whispered,
"You don't really want to know."

"WE DO!"

"Alright," I sighed.
"There's a creature in the basement.
His name is Burback."

A monster?!

"A friendly monster," I said. "He loves children. If you 're kind, he'll come out to see you."

Each night at bedtime, the
girls begged,
"Tell us more about Burback!"

"Please, Daddy," they said.
"Take us to see Burback!"

One Saturday, after work, I finally agreed. "Alright," I said. "We'll visit Burback."

Yay!
Yay!

We took the old service
elevator down,
down,
down,
to the basement.

7 6 5 4 3 2 1 B
RATTLE!
GROAN!

The doors creaked open.
The basement was dark
and echoing.

Then we heard it.
A soft hum, like a lullaby.

"It's Burback," I whispered.
"Don't be afraid.
He won't hurt you."

But the girls squealed!
They darted back into
the elevator.
"Take us up, take us up!"

BEEP!
BEEP!

The doors closed, and we rode back up.

On the way home, the girls whispered. "Did you hear him?

"Did you see his smile?"

They never asked to visit Burbak again. But every night, they dreamed of him, our secret friend in the basement.

Years before Burback

lived in the basement,

I had my own adventure.

It was the summer of

1967.

We dreamed of big houses and big lives. That day, we found a hidden path leading to a deep valley.

And in the valley ...
a cave.

We made a torch, just like
explorers in the movies.
Step by step, we went inside.

Deeper and deeper we went.
Then we heard it-
A low, humming sound.

"Someone lives here," Danny whispered.
We saw benches made of wood, and soft piles like beds.

Suddenly
Clatter!
A stone tumbled
across the floor.

SKITTER

We didn't wait to see
who threw it.
We ran!

All the way out, we laughed and shouted-scared and thrilled at the same time.

We never told anyone.
But I've always
remembered that cave.

And I've always
remembered the sound.

Some say that's where Burback came from - a friendly creature, living quietly, waiting for kind children to visit.

Years later, when my
daughters asked,
I knew exactly what
to say.

And so the story of
Burbak lived on ...

From cave to basement,
from father to daughters,
Burback is always here.

Waiting for kind
children who believe.

THE END

www.ingramcontent.com/pod-product-compliance
Lightning Source LLC
Chambersburg PA
CBHW041223050726
47599CB00001B/58